The mermen were having a game of finball. They had strong tails which they used to flip the ball as they tried to score goals into clam shells. At the sides of the pitch stood some supporters, who were cheering the mermen on.

One little merman, called Sol, was too young to join in so he made up a different game. He had to toss a shell into the waves and his pet dogfish, Chips, had to swim off and bring it back to him.

Sol tossed a shell and it floated into a thick forest of weeds. Chips dashed into the weeds to fetch it. Sol waited, but when Chips did not come back, he swam up to the forest of weeds and called his name.

When Chips still did not come back, Sol swam into the weed forest to look for him. It was green and gloomy there, and the little merman felt afraid.

"Chips!" he called again.

Chips still did not come back but Sol had an odd feeling that something or someone was looking at him. He looked around but there was no one to be seen. He shook his head and swam bravely on.

SNAP went some big, sharp teeth, but Sol did not see them.

Then he spotted a shell, like the one
he had been tossing for Chips, and
ducked down to pick it up.
SNAP went the big, sharp teeth again,
just where Sol had been swimming,
but still he did not see them.

Then Sol spotted a tail sticking out from some weeds. He sped off to see if the tail belonged to Chips.

SNAP went the big, sharp teeth again, just where Sol had been standing, but still he did not see them.

"Chips!" called Sol, as he swam up to where the tail had been. "Chips!" He was just in time to see the tail swimming off. Sol took a deep breath and swam on into the weeds.

SNAP went the big, sharp teeth again, just where Sol had been, but still he did not see them.

Sol was just in time to see the tail shoot into a small hole in the side of a sunken ship. He swam up to it and peeped into the hole. It was dark inside the ship.

"Chips," called Sol softly.

Suddenly, he spotted a long, dark shape waiting in the weeds. The long, dark shape was looking at him and the long, dark shape had big, sharp, snapping teeth!

Sol was terrified and shot into the hole in the side of the sunken ship.

SNAP went the big, sharp teeth again, just outside the hole where Sol had been, but just too late to catch him.

Safe inside the ship, Sol swam to the far corner of the cabin, sat down, and looked around. There was an old cannon, some timbers from the deck, and a chest in one corner.

Then Sol spotted a little head peeping out of the chest.

"Chips!" he called, and Chips slithered out and swam across to Sol. The little dogfish was so happy to see him that he swam around and around his friend until they were quite dizzy.

Sol gave his pet a big hug. Just then, the cabin shook and a pointed nose slammed into the hole in the side of the ship. It was a long nose with big, sharp teeth. It was a shark!

Chips started to shake.
"Help!" Sol called.

The little merman looked around. He tried not to panic, but there was not much time, as the wooden ship was old and the shark was strong.
"Help me!" Sol called to Chips.

Chips helped him to drag the cannon to the hole. The shark tried to ram into the side of the ship again, but this time his pointed snout got stuck inside the cannon.
"Quick!" shouted Sol to Chips. "Swim!"

Sol and Chips swam very quickly. They did not stop until they got safely back to the finball pitch, where the game was just ending. Sol's dad was one of the winners! Sol swam up to him and gave his dad a big hug.

"I am sorry the game took so long," said his dad. "Were you very bored?" Sol gave Chips a quick wink. "Not very," he replied.